Beep Beep
The ROAD RUNNER

™

By Cecily Ruth Hogan
Illustrated by Fred *and* Jill Daunno

A GOLDEN BOOK, New York
Western Publishing Company, Inc., Racine, Wisconsin 53404

D E F G H I J

The Road Runners—Mama Beep, Papa Beep, and the three young Beeps—live in a big sandy desert. The Road Runners belong to a family of special birds who are happiest when they run and run and run.

It's lucky that the Beeps *like* to run, for Wile E. Coyote is always chasing them. He never catches them, though, because they are much too fast.

Today, Wile E. has a new idea. "If I can't outrun those Beeps," he says to himself, "I'll have to trap them!"

The Road Runners are not afraid. After all, they're speedy runners, and they're very smart, too.

Wile E. shakes his fist at the Road Runners. "I'll catch you yet!" he shouts.

Then he rubs his sore foot gently as he starts to plan again. *I'll back them into a cactus,* he decides.

Unlucky Wile E. Coyote! He can't find the Beeps, but he *does* find the cactus spines!

Wile E. is angrier than ever as he pulls
out those stinging cactus spines.

"How can I trap those Beeps if I can't
even find them?" he asks himself. Then he
begins to search again.

The Road Runners see how dirty Wile E. is, so they decide to run toward the water hole. There Wile E. can get washed off while everyone goes for a nice, cool swim.

Wile E. thinks that this is a good idea. "I'll catch them on the lily pad," he says happily, rubbing his paws together.

So the friendly Road Runners toss Wile E. a long rope and, all together, pull him onto the shore.

That nice, cool water makes the Road Runners feel better than ever, but Wile E. feels very muddy and very wet and very tired.

As the Road Runners race off, Wile E. yells to them. "Just you wait until tomorrow!" he says. "I'll get lots of sleep and eat a big breakfast, and I'll be faster than ever!"

But the Road Runners are not worried. They can always get away from Wile E.

Up, down, around, and through—
Wile E. Coyote, we'll outrun you!